The

Revival

BookSquirrel Publication

BookSquirrel Publication

Mahadev Totala Nager, Indore (M.P),452001
Regd Under MSME
Website:
www.booksquirrelpublication.com

"The Revival"

By: Kumari Jyotsna and Amrit Atwal

ISBN: 978-93-89923-15-5

English – Hindi Anthology 1ˢᵗ Edition

Book Formatting: Ishani Agarwal

Cover Design: Ronak Chavda

<u>ACKNOWLEDGEMENT</u>

First and foremost, praises and thanks to the god, the almighty, for his showers of blessings,

The completion of this anthology wouldn't have been possible without the cooperation of all the co-authors, who have put their hard work and efforts, for the success of this anthology.

Big thanks to Kumari Jyostna and Amrit Atwal the compiler and editor who devoted a lot of time and completed the book with full diligence.

Big thanks to our publication team BOOKSQUIRREL PUBLICATION. Extremely grateful for our parents for their love, prayers and sacrifices.

<u>DISCLAIMER</u>

This anthology is a work of fiction. The compilers have tried to make sure that all the write-ups in this book are original and plagiarism free. All the write-ups in this book are unique and belong solely to the respective co-authors. In any case of plagiarism detection neither the publishing house nor the compilers are to be held responsible. The sole responsibility of the write-ups is the respective co-author.

Amrit Atwal

(Compiler)

Amrit Atwal was born in Burnpur,

An industrial city in the state of West Bengal in India. Obsessed with books since childhood, Amrit began penning her own fiction in the eighth grade. When she isn't writing you might find her clicking pictures or drawing a sketch.Visit her on Instagram on @A.Atwalpoetry

<u>COLD</u>

Amrit Atwal

Sun rays rolled down my cheeks.

I looked at the sun

And wished they could reach my heart.

"It's been cold for years" my heart whispered.

<u>NIGHTS LIKE THOSE</u>

Amrit Atwal

Take me back to those nights,

When I slept

Counting the stars,

Not the hours to daylight,

When it was peaceful

Under the sky,

Now the sky feels like

An ocean,

It's too hard to breathe,

It's too numb to feel.

<u>DEAR ME,</u>

Amrit Atwal

I am sorry for all those times,

When clouds choose to rain over you

But you choose to hold

the umbrella for others,

When your body needed your

Arms to hold but you

Choose to hold others,

I am sorry I couldn't

Love you the way

You deserve to be.

Kumari Jyotsna
(Compiler)

Hailing from Bihar, residing in New Delhi,

Jyotsna is a sincere but bubbly girl.

She is a vivid reader and fond of writing poems.

Graduated from Delhi University, Jabra fan of SRK

And a future IAS.

<u>BROKEN VESSEL</u>

Kumari Jyotsna

She is tender sapling bursting besides the odds of

Barren land,

Like a dried fetid flower in some old broken vessels.

Always tried hiding from those harsh thorns, like that

From the abandoned sands.

All those shrewdness of the surrounding world and a

Smile and all get tassels.

The chaos inside the calmness on out,

Atrocious, abhorrent cosmos is surely no good,

For her innocent grin, fragile soul no doubt.

Despite all the servings of the world, all the fetters,

With all the compassion, she never failed to be a glow

Getter.

From which direction to which the wind is blowing,

The world is in some rush,or the earth for a

Moment,not ready for slowing.

The Revival

Leaves meeting to the ground in autumn,

Or springs are marked with the flowers with sheen.

The infant became a handsome adult

After going through all the mischief of teen.

Basically, she wasn't interested or willing to be in all

the chores and worldy fares.

Being busy in the lovely stories, and some lessons

from the characters,

Not in mood to know the folks around, unfolding

layers by layers.

Like distinct, decipherable writing,

Unfortunately calligraphed on some torn discarded.

<u>AN APOLOGY</u>

Monisha Raghunath Dasappa

It's not always easy to say that you are sorry. Despite being remorseful, words don't seem to have the vigor in them to suffice. Too sensitive to look back and probe. It's funny that when you make mistakes, you might not think of it as much of a deal. In fact you tend to outright deny being at fault and take pride in stead. She did the same too. She shred his heart, and threw him to the lurking shadows of dependency. All this while, thinking that it was she that were way too dependent on him. Agreed, he had his flaws and had been mis-stepping too. But, was it really worth jeopardizing and throwing all that was held so close by them, to the packs. Packs of wolves. Potentially rabid, supposedly vicious, indomitable and perfidious wolves. We spend so much of our time in finding faults with someone else, turning a blind eye to all that drew us close in the first instance. Like the perfume bottle eventually running out of it's fragrance. Only if you could pause and breathe, maybe a whiff of essence from the past would hit you soon enough. She was overwhelmed by all that he had put himself into. She couldn't as much stand to think of what was to come. She gave up before she knew that she did. She was scared. It could have been anyone of us. All of us are scared. It could have been the stars re-aligning or the moon eclipsing, but she sought him like he sought her. His arms ached in anticipation of spinning her off her feet and into his embrace. Her soul longed to feast with his in the vicinity again. She was more than sorry that she fought the person and not the problem, he was more than accepting. Her insides twisted and turned in guilt, he soothed her agony. They still and always will have each other. Nothing else mattered.

Guru Ankit singh

खुले आसमां में उड़ता जा रहा था,
किसी ने नजर क्या उठायी जमीं पर आ गिरा।
इस बेदर्द जमाने से मुझे कोई शिकवा नहीं,
जब हमारा ही चलाया हुआ खंजर हम ही पर आ गिरा।

Guru Ankit singh

समझो इन राहो के दर्द को ये भी बयां करती हैं,
ठोकरे देकर लोगो को उनके बोझ को सहा करती हैं।
गम वगैरह तो जिन्दगी के गढ्ढे हैं भर जायेंगें,
यकीन करो राहें संवरने के बाद बिना रूकावटो के चला करती हैं।

Guru Ankit singh

सवाल उम्दा है तो उम्दा जबाव भी होगा,
पूछा है उसने मेरे बारे में तो आया ख्वाब भी होगा।
नाराजगी, हिज़ और बेपरवाई मेरी फितरत में नही,
गर सोचा है बिछुड़ने का तुमने तो मुहब्बत का
हिसाब भी होगा।

<u>THE WORST CURSE</u>

Abhishek Kumar

"I curse you to fall in love with someone",

a broken-heart said.

<u>WHO SAID YOU ARE ALONE?</u>

Ruchi Shukla

When you have serious heartbreak
Or when your life becomes completely opaque.
Who said you are alone?
For your thoughts never left you lone
Even that opaque life reflected light and left an unseen path shone

When you looked high and low for friends around
Or when you searched for happiness abound
Who said you are alone?
For your spirit of quest never left you lone
Even it helped you jump out of your zone.

When you have no one to share you feelings with
Or when the world locked you in your girth
Who said you are alone?
For your soul never left you lone.
Even that locked girth strengthened an invisible bond.

For once on earth
can anyone recall?
Who was left without an escort
by his own self anytime - if at all
you can never leave yourself even if you want
so who will make you alone - when even God can't.

NEVER LET YOURSELF BE TAKEN FOR GRANTED

Shivangi Jaiswal

Just give him few days.. Wait, watch and observe.." See if he comes back". What if I can't wait for a single day? See basically the thing is, you keep running back to him and he gets off and goes to another one.. Because he knows you gonna come back to him.. So why not give him time and make him realize his mistake.. That he is losing you.. "What if he doesn't come back? " So why you wanna be with someone who doesn't love you, is cheating on you and doesn't wanna be with you..

If once somebody leaves you for another one. Never allow them to come back..

" Jo aaj tujhse pyar ka waada karke kisi aur ke sath hai kal voh pata nahi kitno ke sath hoga".

So don't love a person so much that he takes you as a timepass option and changes with time and goes away playing with your emotions...

<u>NEVER LET YOURSELF BE TAKEN FOR GRANTED</u>

Shivangi Jaiswal

Just give him a few days.. Wait, watch and observe.." See if he comes back". What if I can't wait for a single day? See basically the thing is, you keep running back to him and he gets off and goes to another one.. Because he knows you gonna come back to him.. So why not give him time and make him realize his mistake.. That he is losing you.. "What if he doesn't come back? " So why you wanna be with someone who doesn't love you, is cheating on you and doesn't wanna be with you..

If once somebody leaves you for another one. Never allow them to come back..

"Don't trust people who promise to be with you forever yet tomorrow they turn out to be with many more."

So don't love a person so much that he takes you as a timepass option and changes with time and goes away playing with your emotions...

BITTER TRUTH

N Bhavana

No destiny could bring us together.
If that's the way that things are meant to be,
then maybe we'd be better if we never see
each other, 'cause underneath it all,
I'm sick of almost everything.
What do you keep going on about?
You've said and done so many selfish things.
Haven't you taken all that you can take by now?
But even though all that's true,
somehow I can't seem to hate you...
I know...
"I don't wanna' hear you say the same old talk again..."
This time I'll take it all the way to the end!
I don't care if there's a way you phrase it!
"Love me!", "Trust me!", I'll never take it!
If you wanna' fool around, fine with me!
Just don't kid yourself with who you'll never be!
How long will you keep trying?
How many more lying words
you don't even believe?
Either way it'll end, yeah, we already know.
Even if our words aren't our own, I'm tired
of getting my hopes up over nothing at all!
So take the hint! Just take it and don't let my rain fall!
A butterfly out in the world
never sends a text or a call.
It spreads its "wings" out...

Wouldn't you say that way's the greatest of all?
If you don't know what I mean, then just get lost!
If you're that indecisive then just fuck off!
If every word I said never meant a thing-
all the care and thought, it only brought more crying
and pity! If that's true, then maybe
I'll just put my umbrella up after all!
'Cause all that I wanted was to be this way forever,
going on hoping it would get better...
But I was growing older and never
thought I couldn't turn back the clock!
So now, I pray the rain never stops...

<u>FAKE LOVE</u>

N Bhavana

Copy, paste, and delete...
And the pattern repeats...
Take it in... Let it out...
And that is why, becoming someone else's self...
It kills me inside!

I don't care if there's a way you say it!
"Love me!", "Trust me!", I hate it!
If you wanna' fool around, fine by me!
Just don't kid yourself with who we'll never be!
How long will you keep trying?
How many more lying promises I never believed!?

Either way it'll end, yeah, I already know.
Even the words that aren't our own!
I'm tired of hurting each other and myself so much!
So I'll accept the "me" that I became and give it up!

CAN'T DENY LOVE

N Bhavana

Mixed up love and hate
my cherished memories are losing their color
and slipping away slowly
it's deepening day by day
those hurtful words and damaged heart
where is love ?
I tried to avoid it all
I 've tried everything but I can't deny love
too much ego satisfies my hunger
and left me with no compassion
let's try filling it all up again
People come and people go
U and I are standing here
gradually getting used to these muted emotions
my heart is burning up
I'm parched
In trust, I'm filling up this void with you
lighting up a fire in my lifeless heart.

<u>HEARTBREAK AND HEALING</u>

Jaspreet Kaur

Heartbreaks are there to break you
It will take you to world of darkness
Your positivity will turn into negativity
Sadness will take over the role of happiness

You will feel defeated and shattered
You will start to hate being yourself
Things will go against you
What you need just be yourself

What hurts most will heal you
Heartbreaks will get healed slowly
Have some patience and move ahead
Life will go on steadily

Find motivation in your broken past
And rise up as a warrior
Let the pain be healing medicine
For the future you always wanted

<u>WHAT CAN YOU BE GRATEFUL FOR TODAY?</u>

Krishna Thankey

What can you be grateful for today?
For the hidden gems of talents within you
that have started emerging
and are nourishing your soul
with all its glitters,
You have to be grateful.

When you know that
your heart is overflowing with love
because you are spreading love
all around you
And it will continue to serve love
as it is forever boundless,
You have to be grateful.

Experiencing the birth
of a new fragrance within you,
that is bringing a delightful aura
to your soul,
You have to be grateful.

When you are exploring
the beauty within you,
with every cell of your body
painted with the colours
of the Universe,
You have to be grateful.

A STRANGER

Krishna Thankey

It had been many years
and I decided to bestow
my undoubted trust on him.
In the air of love-making
and a close-knit night walk
we reached a secluded hut
with a flickering lamp,
hours of darkness,
and the endless rain.
He looked at me,
with his lustrous eyes.
Shifting closer to my back
he twisted my arms seductively
leaving me out of breath.
I couldn't resist his arts of seduction
which had the power to
dive me in the drive of pleasure.
With the fast passing time
of Lust making,
I could feel
his hands cupping my volcanoes
and his head
between my thighs
making his mouth wet.
Bent on my knees,
I could feel the penetration-
inside me!
Hard and thick
perfectly fitting the void.
The rain outside rhyming with
the sweat moving on my arched back
and my moanings

clashing with the thunder sound.
His horse-like speed,
awakened the tigress in me
uniting the two unknowns
in the world of exotic bliss.
That was not
the end of the wonders
that he gave me
For the next day
he went to the same room
But with a different girl.
Leaving me in a bombshell
and I had no other way
to throw him out of my life
But by giving him the name
of a stranger.

<u>YOU ARE A WINNER</u>
Krishna Thankey

Where are we all heading to?
Probably to the verge of our lives.
Drifting slowly towards the shore
With a burdened heart.
So why to travel
With all the chaos and mess.
Just slow down for a while.
Close your eyes.
Feel the air on your face.
Clutch your fingers.
Scream out of joy.
Bring the powerful vibes within you.
Kindle your blissful heart
Sing, while you attract people
to join you
in the mystical marathon of life.
The marathon where you vow to
tell the people around
That the world is beautiful
If they choose to
See the good things that it carries.
Walk slowly on the crooked lanes
With enormous confidence and a smile.
Let the waves smash you
but keep standing wide and firm
And you will eventually
Experience the Life itself
bowing down in front of you.
Trust yourself
For you are a winner
If you choose to.

अधूरी कहानी

Ultimate Loser

कुछ अलग सी थी हमारी कहानी

वो आग थी और मैं था पानी

पूरी होनी ही न थी हमारी कहानी

कुछ यूं बदला उसने मुझको बेपरवाह से मुझको

दे दी नई ज़िंदगानी

कुछ अलग सी थी हमारी कहानी

मिलना भी था और नहीं भी

ये भी थी शायद उस ख़ुदा की निगहबानी

लकीरों में था मिलना लिखा पर

बिछड़ गए सुनकर दिमाग की ज़ुबानी

कुछ अलग सी थी हमारी कहानी

प्यार तो बेशुमार था हम दोनों में

लेकिन झगड़ो की भी अपनी अलग रवानी

कुछ अलग सी थी हमारी कहानी

वो आग थी और मैं था पानी

मिलते तो खत्म कर देते किसी एक की कहानी

<u>इज़हार</u>

Ultimate Loser

कैसे करें इज़हार-ए-मोहब्बत

ये खेल बड़ा निराला हैं

बहुतेरे आशिक़ों का इसने

पल में जनाज़ा निकाला है

अधूरे इश्क़ की दास्तानों का

इस जग में रहा बोलबाला है

कैसे करें इज़हार-ए-मोहब्बत

ये खेल बड़ा निराला हैं

अपनी ज़ुल्फो के जाल में

इस दिल को तूने फ़सा डाला है

क़ातिल निगाहों ने तेरी

इस दिल को मार डाला है

कैसे करें इज़हार-ए-मोहब्बत

ये खेल बड़ा निराला हैं

चाय

Ultimate Loser

सुख में चाय,

दुःख में चाय;

चाय ने अनेकों रिश्ते बनाए ।

पढ़ाई की चिंता, प्यार में धोखा;

चाय ने था हर गम को रोका ।

बिछड़ा हुआ वो यार पुराना,

या फिर हो प्यार का फ़साना;

नए लोगों से रिश्ते बनाए ।

ये चाय ही हैं दोस्त जो;

दुश्मनों को भी पास लाए ।

उन हसीन लम्हों को फिर से जिएँ;

आओ चाय पिएँ...।

ज़िन्दगी के उन खूबसूरत लम्हों को फिर से जिएँ,

जब मिलते थे चार यार होती थी बातें हज़ार;

चाय की अड़ी पर वो दुनिया फिर से जिएँ, आओ चाय पिएँ ।

LOVE IS LONELY

Zeeshan Rizvi

ये तोहफा ईश्क ने हमको दिया है..

तबाह ज़िन्दगी इसने किया है.

. मोहब्बत की है तो पछताओ तुम अब..

ये बला है जो तुमने सर लिया है..

हर इक दर्दों को जामो मे मिलाके..

तेरा ही नाम लेकर बस पिया है..

मरहम भी वो लगा रहा है मुझको..

मोहब्बत का ज़खम जिसने दिया है..

तू जब तक साथ थी मेरे तो तब तक..

हर ईक लम्हा खुशी से ही जिया है..

मेरे बेसाख्ता आंसू है निकले..

वफ़ा का ज़िक्र जिसने भी किया है..

मेरी तनहाईयों से पूछ जाकर..

हर ईक ज़ख्मो को हाथों से सिया है..

तजुर्बा ईश्क का ज़ीशान ये है..

सुकूनो चैन इसने बस लिया है..

THE KEY TO MY HEART

Zeeshan Rizvi

तेरे सितम की सनम सबको जानकारी है..

तेरे सितम पे मगर मेरा ईश्क भारी है..

निचोड़ लेता है रूह को ये जिस्म से लोगों..

यही है ईश्क यही ईश्क की बीमारी है..

जो दे रहा था सदा साथ उम्र भर देगा..

पसन्द उसको फ़कत अब ये दुनियादारी है..

ज़मीर अपना मैं दौलत के लिए क्यूँ बेचूँ..

बची ये दिल मे मेरे इतनी तो खुददारी है..

जो गिर भी जाऊँ तो मुझको संभाल लेगा कोई.

. बनाई इसलिये यारों से हमने यारी है..

छिड़ा था ज़िक्र कभी तेरा बीच महफिल में..

तो मैने कह दिया यारों गज़ल हमारी है..

किसी से ईश्क हुआ और किसी ने ईश्क किया..

अजीब रस्म है दुनिया की मगर प्यारी है..

करीब दिल के जो आया तो वो चला भी गया..

लुटा हूँ आज मैं तो कल किसी की बारी है..

जो कभी कट नहीं सकती थी तेरे बाद सनम..

वही एक उम्र मैने उम्र भर गुज़ारी है..

मुखालिफो को मैं ज़ीशान राख कर दूँगा..

कलम में मेरे अभी इतनी तो चिंगारी है

<u>WARRIOR</u>

Zeeshan Rizvi

ये बन्दा सर उठाना जानता है..

झुकाना गर ज़माना जानता है..

अगर तुम होश मे हो तो ये सुनलो..

मोहब्बत होश उड़ाना जानता है..

तेरी आँखों मे ही बस डूबता दिल..

नशे का ये ठिकाना जानता है..

मुसलसल ज़ख्म लगते जा रहे है..

मगर दिल मुस्कुराना जानता है..

बहोत से राज़ सीने में दफन है..

मेरा दिल सब छुपाना जानता है..

इरादा नेक तुम करके तो देखो..

तुम्हे रब जगमगाना जानता है..

सवार ईश्क की कश्ती मे ना हो..

ये बन्दो को डुबाना जानता है..

भरोसा तुम खुदा पे करके देखो..

भरोसा वो निभाना जानता है..

कलम में खून की सियाही को भरके..

गज़ल ज़ीशान लिखना जानता है..

<u>ARE YOU THERE?</u>

Ritika Dasgupta

Are you there?
I've been searching
I've been looking.
But I can't anymore.

Can you come?
I've been holding in a lot.
I've been pretending a lot.
But I can't anymore.

Can you see me?
They say you're gone forever.
But I say you're somewhere near.
I just can't find you.

Can you hear?
The beat of my heart
Now beating for the both of us.
I can't take it anymore.

Can you feel?
The wind blowing outside.
Are you hiding there?
Just tell me where.

Can't you see?
I'm getting tired now.

I'm slowly giving in now.
Just tell me once.

Don't you understand?
I don't wanna face it alone.
I don't wanna go on anymore.
I need you so bad.

There tears dry by their own
And you're not here
to wipe them anymore.
You're not here to make me smile.
These people keep on saying
That you're not coming back.
But I'll just sit here and wait for you,
Till i close my eyes forever
And dream of you.

मोहब्बत थी हमारी

Auchitya Saini

मोहब्बत थी हमारी,

तुमने नाकाम की है

धोखा देकर हमें

बेज्जती हमारी सरेआम की है

फिर भी अब तक हमारी मौजूदगी की तलाश करता हूं

नफ़रत करने के बावजूद, बस तुमसे प्यार करता हूं||

तुमसे शुरुआत की है

Auchitya Saini

तुमसे शुरुआत की है

तुम पर अब भी अटका

जमाना काफी आगे बढ़ गया है

पर अब भी मैं तुम्हारे लिए रुका हुआ हूं

नहीं अपनी कोई तारीफ नहीं कर रहा

बस प्यार दिखा रहा हूं

एक तरफा ही सही प्यार का रिश्ता है

अभी वह बस अकेले ही निभा रहा हूं

कोशिश है कभी तो तुम भी ध्यान दोगी

कि तुम्हारे लिए मैं जमाने से बिछड़ता जा रहा हूं

तुम्हारी एक मुस्कुराहट के लिए मैं मरता जा रहा हूं

MAIN ADALAT MAIN KHADA HOON

Dr Tilak Dixit

कहने को मैं बेगुनाह मैं हूं

अदालत में खड़ा हूं

आरोपों से मैं बना हूं

वह बोलते हैं मैं

सफाई दिया करता हूं

मुझे आज तक यही लगा

मैं सच बोला करता हूं

पत्थरों की बारिश में

शीशे का छाता लिए खड़ा हूं

कहने को मैं बेगाना हूं

मैं अदालत में खड़ा हूं

दूसरी और बो जानता है

जिनका मैं कसूरवार हूं

मैं अपनी तरफ से अकेला ही खड़ा हूं

मुकदमा बरसो चलेगा

अब तो जीत को भी आने लगा हूं

सजा को अब साथी मानता हूं

क्योंकि कर्तव्य निभाया करता हूं

कहने को मैं बेगुनाह हूं

मैं अदालत में खड़ा हूं||

I SHUT MY EYES

Dr Tilak Dixit

I shut my eyes
So that I can walk in my dream
Free from areas of scream
I walk around with passion
And collect the fallen compassion

I shut my eyes
To open a new gate
Where I met my fate
I greet
But he greed

I shut my eyes
Where past remain past
I restart my future
And run the task

EMPTINESS

Dr Tilak Dixit

Today after a step up I realised
That I can hear a sound
As if someone was talking from behind
I saw some of the finest above me
But I was shock to see
What emptiness looks like
As it talks like me.

HUNGRY

Sampurna Ghosh

You studied the things I love the most,
Then invited me to have it for free.
I should've realized, should've known that's what you do:
You invite the mouse to have its cheese.

SAVIOUR

Sampurna Ghosh

There were demons in all of my rooms,
My mind was flooding,
My soul was drowning,
And the cold water was freezing my blood.
They all threw me life boats, ropes,
stretched out their hands,
hoping I don't get a grip,
And take them down with myself,
That's when you came:
With literally nothing,
You looked at me and screamed,
"Let's teach you swimming".

<u>TRUSTING THE DARK</u>

Sampurna ghosh

And that's the problem with me ..
When I love someone,
I love them so much that
when they run away,
I don't chase them,
nor do I shut my gates,
I sit there, believing
They've gone for a run

<u>MY DEAR LOVE</u>

Bhavana Chinni

You left me like a passing cloud;
beautiful only till a moment.

I choose to respect my love and distanced myself from you; but at
what cost? Asks the heart.

It still feels the same, without you around. I don't feel like I've kept
an end to you.

Ask me why? Because, my little foolish heart still hopes for the
hopeless love; still wishes you to message me back; still beats till
the breath of my life, as long as you're in it.

INHALE AND EXHALE

Bhavana chinni

Inhale, let that pain sink in.
Let every feeling of the desperation to be loved back sink in.
Let all the glitters of day dreaming flattered apart sink in.
Let the exhausted death of every night, in where you've shuttered
your heart sink in.
Let the cosy imagination lingering in your mind sink in.
Let this process of healing sink in.
Inhale, let the pain sink in.
Exhale, let it go.

DEAR SELF

Bhavana chinni

Don't be soo hard on yourself today. I know it still hurts like hell.
But, I promise things will surely get better. Never underestimate
yourself to be weak. Because, I know what you've been through
and I really do understand how painful it is for you to succumb the
pill of rejection. I am with you in this bad phase; hand in hand.
Let's heal slowly.

मोहब्बत को रुस्वा

Rohit Singh

यूँ मेरी मोहब्बत को रुसवा करके,

तुम्हे सुकूँ नहीं मिलेगा, ओ सितमगर !

तुमने मेरी मोहब्बत को ठुकराया हैं, जाओ !

तुम्हे भी तुम्हारा प्यार नहीं मिलेगा।

ये कैसी कश्मकश हैं

Rohit Singh

ये कैसी कश्मकश हैं ज़िन्दगी ? यू तो हमे उनसे मोहब्बत हैं,

मगर इस बात से उन्हें बग़ावत हैं,

जब मुकम्मल नहीं हैं उनका मिलना हमे,

फिर इस दिल को उनकी चाहत क्यों हैं?

कहाँ से लाओगी

Rohit Singh

प्यार तो तुम्हे हर किसी का मिल जाएगा,

लेकिन ये ज़ुनून कहाँ से लाओगी?

जो सुकून था मोहब्बत में मेरे,

वो सुकून कहाँ से लाओगी?

POWER OF SELF

Deepti

God gives power to see at night,
Depends on you finding the light.

Turning point comes when heart mind fight,
Intellect defeats them wisely use might.

Despite all hurdles be like Dwight,
Analyze the trouble with keen sight.

Passion will surely lead you right,
Faith always makes your future bright.

Build self-trust to get height,
Be optimistic to achieve success delight.

Grab opportunities catch the ball,
There are possibilities you may fall.

Make your body begin to crawl,
Never give up stop to bawl.

People who hurt you do brawl,
Get rid of those by showing lol.

Do not make your destiny scrawl,
You must deserves best of all.

Thank everybody who give catcall,
Now it's time to break stonewall.

22ND APRIL 2018 ,THE TALE OF MY COMEBACK

Saswat Baral

3rd Standard: 1st Suicide Attempt
6th Standard: 2nd Suicide Attempt
10th Standard: 3rd Suicide Attempt
11th Standard: 2 Suicide Attempts
Before Dropping Diploma 1st Year: 6th Suicide Attempt

This was the day in 2018 I understood that when my own people didn't understand me, didn't care me the way I have thought of, then why should I care for them and sacrifice my life.

I have learnt to be happy, I have learnt to fail, I have loved to be a failure, I have learnt to smile even in depressing times, I have to wake up I have learnt to be Strong, I have learnt to be Bold, I have learnt to be Audacious, with everyday passing by,I have been learning to wake up and stand up tall after getting crushed and thrashed. I am becoming stronger and stronger.

I got to know my worth, I got to know my importance, this was the way I learnt to be brave and valiant.

It Was A Day,
I Went To Railway Station,
To Return Back Home,
In Small Cut Pieces Of My Body Parts,
But Returned Back Home,
By Uniting And Glueing,
My Broken Pieces Of Heart

AFTERSHOCK

Tarun Jeevnani

My heartbeat was crumbled,
I felt a shock go through my body,
I saw my life being scrambled across the floor,
everywhere was just pain and agony.

I learnt a great deal of lesson,
not to love and not to trust,
to love makes me vulnerable,
and everyone begins to break my trust.

I am enjoying this singular phase of mine,
as I have no reason to smile,
I enjoy myself for I cannot deceive me,
there is a piece of you still inside me.

It talks to me when I am lonely,
I make up fantasies to ignore you,
the truth is I miss you,
and this truth is unbearable.

I control my emotions,
I keep them at bay,
for I remain alone,
it's my purpose nowadays.

I hate these relationship,
who are weak and confusing,
I enjoy the voice of nature,
as it reaches my soul and is soothing.

<u>TWO OF US!</u>

Atharva Bhoyarkar

You used to call me my sun and stars and I used to refer

to you as the moon of my life.

We wanted a love story as strong as the one Khaleesi and Khal
Drogo had.

A love story that will make us stronger, one that no human being
could destroy.

But we were wrong our love story wasn't,

It was nothing close to strong

It disappeared as shallow as it came along and it easily got
destroyed by two human beings,

Or maybe a little more.

Little have we known that Khaleesi and Drogo's love wasn't
immortal?

Unfortunately for the lovebirds we were, it was.

So I hope you'll always remember this,

When the sun rises in the west and sets in the east Then you
should return to me my sun and stars

आधुनिक मानव

Ram Prakash

इस ज़माने का हुआ आज ऐसा हाल है । हर किसी की बात में कोई ना कोई चाल है ।। सुख सुविधा है विपुल मन अभाव से घिरा । आडंबर ग्रस्त मनुज वास्तविकता से गिरा । स्वार्थमय अनीति से तनिक व्यक्ति न डरा । व्यर्थ ही निज भूल से जीवन जहर से भरा । आभा मंडित था कभी वेदनामय भाल है । हर किसी की बात में कोई ना कोई चाल है ।। मन में प्रपंच और वाणी में मिठास । देखने में लगता है अपना कोई खास । मौके पर देता हमको वही त्रास । आज हमदर्द का नहीं विश्वास । वाक्-पटुता अब बनी छल कपट का जाल है । हर किसी की बात में कोई ना कोई चाल है ।। मनुष्य आज जल रहा द्वेष की आग में । हर कोई खोया हुआ व्यर्थ के राग में । आदमी के गुण हुए होते जैसे नाग में । चाँदनी को भुला दिया चाँद के दाग में । अज्ञान के तूफान से ज्ञान हुआ कंगाल है । हर किसी की बात में कोई ना कोई चाल है ।। मर्यादाहीन राजनीती फैला भ्रष्टाचार । हृदय हुए ज्वालामुखी व्यास हा हा कार । नेता सत्तावान हैं जनता पर अत्याचार । देशद्रोही दानवों ने फैलाया अनाचार । सत्ता लोलुपताओं ने किया देश हलाल है । हर किसी की बात में कोई ना कोई चाल है ।। संकीर्णता विश्वासघात वर्तमान की भ्यंकार ज्वाला । डसता बनकर नाग वही दूध पिलाकर जिसको पाला । अपना बनकर आज मनुष्य अपनों के ही मारे भाला । मानवता को स्वयं मनुज ने आज गहन संकट में डाला । आचरण के तिमिर में आह का जन्जाल है । हर किसी की बात में कोई ना कोई चाल है ।। अहंकार त्यागकर स्वार्थपरता मार दो । ईर्ष्या को छोड़कर भावनामय प्यार दो । प्रेरणा

को बाँटकर जनजीवन संवार दो । प्रज्ञामय ज्ञान का समाज को उपहार दो । मानव की जिंदगी का सदाचरण ढाल हो । हर किसी की बात में कोई ना कोई चाल है ।। कुप्रथायें भूलकर नारी को सम्मान दो । बच्चों को नित्यप्रति नैतिक सद्ज्ञान दो । अपराधों का हनन कर देश को मुस्कान दो । अनीतियों का दमन कर इन्सान की पहचान दो । जिंदगी की राह में मौत का ख़याल हो । हर किसी की बात में कोई ना कोई चाल है ।। संयम को साधकर उन्मादों पर ताला दो । प्यार को बाँटकर स्नेह सुरभित माला दो । संस्कृति अपनाकर अमृतमय प्याला दो । तिमिर को मिटाकर सुखमय उजाला दो । "दीप" के त्योहार में अँधेरे का मलाल हो । हर किसी की बात में कोई ना कोई चाल है ।।

दस्तूर अधूरी मुहब्बत का--- ज़ख्म भरेंगे जरूर

Shivam Tiwari

नज़रों से नज़रें मिली ना मिली,

आंखों में उसके नूर था, उसके लिए था

इंसान मैं अजनबी, औरों में मैं मशहूर था।

उसका यूं मुस्कुराना बेवजह, रेशमी जुल्फों को संवारना,

जी करता उसकी इबादत करूं, दिल में इतना जुनून था।

धड़कनों के करीब सजाया उसको, मैं उससे कहीं दूर था,

किस तरह उसका दीदार करूं, यह सोचने को मजबूर था।

इक दिन जुबां पर आ ही गया, एहसास जो दिल में भरा था,

इश्क़ जो होना था सो हो गया, इसमें मेरा क्या कुसूर था।

कुछ ना कहा बस उलझाए रखा, मेरा प्यार उसे नामंज़ूर हुआ,

कैसे सुनाऊं दास्तां तुमको, दिल टूटकर चकनाचूर हुआ।

चाह कर भी चाहत मिल ना सकी, यही था नसीब में शायद,

लैकिन लिखा था जो तकदीर में मेरे, बेशक मुझे वो मंज़ूर हुआ।

आज भी ख्यालों में झलक उठता है,

उस चेहरे से छलकता नूर,

अरसे बीत गए इन बातों को, कभी ज़ख्म ये भरेंगे जरूर।

मुकम्मल हो न सका इश्क़,

चाहा था दिलोंजान से "शिवम्", अधूरी मुहब्बत थी एक तरफ की,

है कुछ ऐसा इसका दस्तूर।

<u>MY BESTFRIEND WAS A TREE</u>

Prabhnoor Kaur Dhaliwal

It's no more...still in my memories it's alive
I knew it since i was five
Though there were many like it
But only under it's shade I liked to sit
It didn't belonged to me,
But it was something I loved to see
You must be thinking who is 'it'
It was where I felt lit
It was with whom I shared everything
It was with whom I ones loved to sing
It provided me life in form of Oxygen
In every season
It was and always will be my best friend
But it's life came to an end
It was a tree in my neighbour's park
Which was cut in the last night's dark
Some might think that I'm insane
Because they can't understand my pain
But I have to heal
Also, I need to feel
feel it's presence in many more
That will grow from the earth's core.

A MOTHER WHO LOST HER MOTHER

Prabhnoor Kaur Dhaliwal

Black Maskara being mixed with her tears,
Rolling down her cheeks along with her fears.
Dropping on her white dress,
Slowly releasing all her stress.

Her mom left her with a broken heart,
And remainings of her art.
Her mom made her life the best,
and herself went for a permanent rest.

No one can take her mom's place,
But she's not alone going through this phase.
Her daughter Annie,
Too lost her granny.

Till now even a single word was not spoken,
Still they knew the girl was broken.
Atleast for the little girl she had to heal,
and with the situation she had to deal .

Sagar Balasaheb Bhandare

दिन गुजर गया अब शाम होने को है,

बिना दीदार के उसके ये आंखे रोने को है,

बादल भी गरज उठे मेरी सांसो मे , लगता है

इस दिल में तुफान आनें को है।

इतना कमजोर तो ना था,

शायद मन उदास होने को है,

कुछ उसकी माजबुरीया होंगी ,कूछ नादानीया,

अब तो खुदा ही जाने आनेवाली इस रात की सुबाह कब होने को है।

Sagar Balasaheb Bhandare

कुछ उम्मीद लगाए बैठा हूँ

एक ख़्वाब आँखो में सजाए बैठा हूँ

बस ये वक़्त अभी मेरा नहीं वरना मैं तो

जश्न कीं तैयारी किए बैठा हूँ।

Sagar Balasaheb Bhandare

कुछ पुराने ज़ख़्म हैं

जिन्हें आज कुरेदना चाहता हूँ,

मैं अपनी कलमसे तुम्हारा नाम लिखना चाहता हूँ।

जिन्हें आज कुरेदना चाहता हूँ,

ALMIGHTY'S GREATEST CREATION, HUMAN

(Saeraa.S) Bushra Shaikh

Almighty's Greatest Creation, Human

"Life is a mess,
Life is miserable,
Life is full of ups and down,
Life is a survival,
Life is an exam,
Life is not easy to live".

Hearing to all these unpleasant terms life said,

Why do you keep pulling Life into your mess,
Why do you keep calling Life with such vacuous names,
What have I even done,
What is my fault if you don't know how to deal with things,
What have I got to do with it,
You never asked me while taking decisions,
So why complain.

Situation are not created by Life,
But are created in Life,
It is created on the decision made my you Human,
So why blame Life,
Why curse Life,
I am baring you human as much as you are baring me,
So why complain.

You were given Life to live it your way,
You have your free-will,
Living Life to the fullest is also in your hands,
When someone asks you human,
How is life,

You keep saying it's doing fine, don't ask,
Why, have Life been so difficult on you Human,
Or have you been so difficult on yourself.

Human this Life which you keep cribbing about is a blessing,
If you take a step in my direction,
I'll take two steps towards you,
Any how you'll have to stay with me,
So why not happily,
Human beings are the Almighty's greatest creation,
Know your worth,
Don't waste it in grumbling.

"Life living on Earth is a blessing,
Human is the Almighty's greatest creation,
Don't grumble,
Learn to live it,
Know the worth of the Life given"

Vaidehi Kathote

Some things never change. They say time heals everything; but it is not always True! The only thing that changes with time is our level of Perception. They say situation change as the time passes. But I think situation forces US to change; time being constant. Poor Us. It is not always our fault but sometimes it is the situation too.

You believe that you feel comfortable with me, I know that I'm secure with you & we both know that we are the Happiest when are together. That's what matters the most

You know when I'm alone some songs remind me of you which we once sung together. Some streets remind me of you where we had been many times together. Some random dialogues/statements remind me of you which you had once said to me. Now, they won't change as the time passes by & I will make sure they won't.

Everybody is free to make their choices. We did the same. We choose to be together. #together forever. We very well know that our present choices will ultimately affect our future & we are ready for the same.

Somewhere I expected that I too should have someone with whom I can share my daily chores, share my darkest secrets, cry my lungs out, pour my Heart out & what not!

Love was not at all a part of my vocabulary. But you introduced me to that romantic world in which only you are my Hero!

Instead of giving up on me, you calmly handled my mood swings.

Instead of complaining, you happily fulfilled my every single demand.

Instead of stopping me to fly, you encouraged me to achieve my dreams.

The way you explained me that," No matter what, we will never let rumors create misunderstanding between US. Don't stop talking to me; because You mean everything to me. I can replace everything in my Life except You".

I love the way you convinced me that, "We will sort out every complicated issue by discussing them & won't argue for silly reasons".

Your way of advising me to follow my diet was way too adorable. "Crushes are temporary, YOU are permanent" made me laugh out louder. You controlled yourself when you badly needed me on those days when I could barely tolerate a single touch on my body. I'm sorry for that, it was not at all intentional. You knew your limits very well & acted accordingly.

We know that we are not going to face the happy phase forever. Problems are definitely going to be there. Some might get jealous of Us, some might test our bond, some might test our honesty; but the Trust YOU had on ME made me fall in Love for you again Yes, I do have weird mood swings but I know You & only You can handle me & calm me down.

I love you because when I'm in the bad mood & you do weird things to make me smile.

I love you because you always take efforts to make me feel special. I love you more when you kiss me on my forehead & say," Don't worry, Baby! I'm here with you ALWAYS. Whenever you feel low, just close your eyes keep your hand on your Heart & I will run through your mind; which will sooth your Soul & be pleasurable to you"

You know why I have such intense feelings for you because you are always in an attempt to make me feel relax, to satisfy me, to make me feel happier than I ever was!

You fought for my dreams when you were busy fighting yours! From a properly dressed girl to a messy haired girl; you loved me to the core irrespective of my look. I should say that "In the lust craving world you were the only person you craved for my soul"& I love that more.

Many a times I slept on your shoulder while you were talking to me but instead of blaming me for not listening you; you let me sleep there.

You wanted me to express my love for you so I started writing. I try to arrange my feelings in these 26 alphabets but something is

left always. Your beauty is beyond words my love
There is always an attempt to do so but I can't totally express it
here, because writing these feelings would be like limiting them
but I don't want that.. My love is limitless..!!
In every mysterious & magical way you created an aura that still
have a deep impact on my Soul!
Yes, I love you not because of your physical beauty but with your
inner beauty.
Yes, I love you & will always do in every possible way.
Here I take a vow that I will respect you & your family & will love
them too taking your complete responsibility.
Honestly I never knew LOVE but you built my faith on Love. And
now I proudly say this that Yes. I DO LOVE YOU FOR MANY
REASONS!
I'm much more fortunate to have you. I Thank Almighty daily for
sending you to me.
You are a miracle to me my Darling!
#my_wonderful_miracle
I LOVE YOU

Bikash Prasad Mahato

कलीफ-ए-मौत होती है वह अल्फाज

जब पता हो कि वह अल्फाज तुमने कहीं हो।

Bikash Prasad Mahato

कोई समझे ना समझाएं उस बेपिर को,

क्योंकि जिंदगी ने उसे खूब अच्छे से समझाया है।

THE CHAOS

Sunit Agarwal

The chaos in my heart,
Calls for your name every time,
The chaos in my mind,
Silently pretend to be fine,

The chaos in my ears,
Hear you name everywhere,
The chaos in my eyes,
Finds everything fare,

The chaos in my skin,
Can feel your love even at distance,
The chaos in my tongue,
Got your taste at one glance,

The chaos in my legs,
Walks upto you for you seem like a magnet to me
The chaos in my hands,
Spreads for a warm hug,

The chaos in my body wants you,
For like a wind you flew.

SHADOW OF THE PAST

Sunit Agarwal

No matter how far I travel in the future,
The past always take a space in my mind,
After since I met you, the life after then is a venture
Only darkness is the place where peace I can find

But then even in the black
There's little light, enough to display
The shadow of my past,
Keeps reminding me of incidents so vast,

But, even in the diverse incidents,
Mistakes spotted were so tiny,
Yet enough to be noticed and end up everything
Leaving with my heart no more to sing,

But, even the silence was so loud
To keep my overhead full of dark clouds
Yet they never rained,
Just to wash my past that was shadow instead.

तड़पते देखा है

अम्बिकेश कुमार 'चंचल'

मैंने, उसे तड़पते देखा है
आँखों को डूबते देखा है
भारतेन्दु की माधुरी में -
गाते देखा है
हिय के दर्द में हृदय को
मैंने, उसे तड़पते देखा है

पथ निहारत नयनों को
न थकते देखा है
फैलते हुए आँचल को
न फैलाते देखा है
सुत-आसुत जल में समाते देखा है
हिय के दर्द में हृदय को
मैंने, उसे तड़पते देखा है

भूले-बिसरे आँसुओं को
फिर से बहते देखा है
अश्क़ पटों को कभी
न सूखते देखा है
मिलन की आस में विरह को ठगते देखा है
हिय के दर्द में हृदय को

मैंने, उसे तड़पते देखा है

पांवों के छालों को देखा है
रिसते हुए घावों को देखा है
सजते हुए मिलन के अरमानों को देखा है
कायनात के पार ख्वाबों को
सत्य में बदलते देखा है
हिय के दर्द में हृदय को
मैंने, उसे तड़पते देखा है

अम्बिकेश कुमार 'चंचल'

मोहब्बत हमारी इतनी निकम्मी है
तुम दिल न दुखाते तो क्या करते।

इश्क करती है, मगर भूल जाती है
तुम फितरत इंसानी न दिखाते तो क्या करते।

फलक पर सजाया था, हलक से निकाल लाया
तुम जमीं न दिखाते तो क्या करते।

माना कि बेवफाई में रगों की मजबूरियाँ रही होंगी
हम आँखों में नमीं न दिखाते तो क्या करते।

दुनिया ने सिखाए हैं फायदों के गुर इतने
तुम रिश्ते में सौदेबाजी न करते तो क्या करते।

दाँव शातिर हर पल खेला गया अंजान के साथ
खेल से हम खुद को न हटाते तो क्या करते।

मोहब्बत हमारी इतनी निकम्मी है
तुम दिल न दुखाते तो क्या करते।

BIO

&

PICTURES

Monisha Raghunath Dasappa
IG: _monisha_dasappa_
This is Monisha Raghunath Dasappa, hailing from Bangalore. Twenty something doctor to be and a poet at heart. Would like to augment her writing enough to call herself Ms. Caroline Rozario's protege, someday.

Guru Ankit Singh
IG:guru_shayri

Ambikesh Kumar Chancha
IG: ambikeshkc
I am a commerce graduate from BHU, and SEO, Content Writer, Web Designer by Profession. Writing is my passion. I am from Varanasi.

Abhishek Kumar
IG: he_is_the_lover.11
I am a student of Class XI and presently studying in Adamas International School. I like to read story books and write quotes.

Ruchi Shukla
IG: __iamruchi__
The passionate poetess, born on 6th May 2001 ,
stepped into the cosmos of poetry at a young
age of thirteen .

Shivangi Jaiswal
IG: the_knockingvibe
Shivangi Jaiswal is from kolkata. She is doing
her post graduation in finance. A writer by day
and reader by night. She loves to bring smiles
and hapiness to many faces, so she is into
social service.

N Bhavana
IG: _im_anny19
Bhavana N, hailing from vizag , student
pursuing doctor of pharmacy , Passionate about
writing.

Jaspreet Kaur
IG_kaur_jaspreet_
This is Jaspreet Kaur. I have Keen interest in
writing poetry. Good at conveying
philosophical ideas and motivational thoughts.

Krishna Thankey
IG: Krishnathankey389
I am Krishna Thankey, an Indian, exploring English Literature. Being an ambivert, I have created my own flawless world.

Ultimate loser
IG: @ultimate__loser
I Ultimate looser,I'm born and bought up in a city where people come to die, The holy city of Lord Shiva 'Kashi' aka Varanasi. I started writing a few months ago.

Zeeshan Rizvi
IG: kalamkaar.01
Zeeshan Rizvi was born in Betul a Green City in the state of Madhya pradesh in India. He is a poet, Writer and a good snooker player.

Ritika Dasgupta
IG: Ritzy_grey
she is Ritika Dasgupta. She started with English hons. and afterwards took up psychology. She is the co- author of the world's thinnest anthology.

Auchitya Saini
IG: Auchityasaini_1408
Auchitya saini was born in New Delhi, India in 2000. Started his write-ups from his 7th standard.Auchitya saini mainly writes poetry on heartbreaks, and the matters that effect society that need a special attention.

Dr. TilakDixit
IG: Right2write_the_left
Dr Tilak Dixit is a practicing physician in Udaipur . He has keen interest in writing metaphoric writeups. He has been part of various anthologies and competitions.

Sampurna Ghosh
IG: sam_g________
Sampurna Ghosh, 17 years old, writes songs, composes music and fears needles. Lives in Kolkata, West Bengal. Plays the piano sometimes, likes biology!

Bhavana Chinni
IG: inside_us_quotes
Hi everyone! This is Bhavana Chinni from Visakhapatnam, Andhra Pradesh. I'm currently pursuing my MBA program and I'm quite passionate about writing

Rohit Singh

मेरा नाम रोहित सिंह हैं मेरा जन्म उत्तर प्रदेश के प्रसिद्ध जिले वाराणसी में हुआ और मैं यही पला-बड़ा हूँ। मैं कोई भी लेख बहुत प्यार और दृढता से लिखने की कोशिश करता हूँ।

Deepti
IG: rvjd_arts

I am Deepti (Owner of business Rvjd Creations, Artist and Poetess). I love to convey my feelings and share my experiences to inspire others through my self made bilingual poems.

Saswat Baral

This Is Saswat Baral, Age 20, Resident Of Rourkela Steel City, Odisha.Hobbies:Writing, Music, Cricket, Football And Kabbadi. Role Models: Rahul Dravid And Cristiano Ronaldo

Atharva Bhoyarka
IG: _thewordaddictbong_

Atharva Bhoyarkar Basically from Nagpur, the city of oranges is a boy named Atharva Bhoyarkar. He loves to portray his emotions and thoughts on the paper in the form of poems. He is a protest poet (the person who address to real socio-political issues and express objection against them).

Ram Prakash
IG: rvjdcreations
This is Ram Prakash "Deep" (Retired Central Govt. Gazetted Officer, Engineer [AMIE India] and Poet. I started writing poems since 1981 and also shared stages with various national level poets.

Shivam Tiwari
IG: shivam 1371
शिवम् तिवाड़ी, राजस्थान की ऐतिहासिक नगरी बीकानेर के निवासी है। वर्तमान में जवाहरलाल नेहरू कृषि विश्वविद्यालय, जबलपुर में स्नातकोत्तर स्तर के विद्यार्थी है ।

Prabhnoor Kaur Dhaliwal
IG: dhaliwal_pk
Prabhnoor Kaur Dhaliwal was born in moga city in the Indian state of Punjab.She is a 17 year old class 12 medical student. Her hobbies are photography and reading books.

Sagar Balasaheb Bhandare
IG: el__oceano
Sagar Balasaheb Bhandare He is basically from a small town of Maharashtra 'SANGLI' which is known as NATYA PANDHARI (land of drama). He is an aspiring writer and willing to spread happiness through his thoughts.

Vaidehi Kathote
A budding doctor in making who loves to express her feeling through her writeups, poems & a strong believer of KARMA!

(Saeraa.S) Bushra Shaikh
Saeraa. S, is pursuing degree in Mechanical Engineering, she's also a Pranic Healer and Meowther to her six cats. She's an animal lover, likes to read suspense and write on philosophy

Bikash Prasad Mahato
Curious soul with enthusiastic spirit.....more realistic person then being in fantasy

Sunit Agarwal
IG: the_ugly_words
He is Sunit Agarwal from Pakyong Sikkim India a business and his hobbies are coin collection, writing, drawing and cooking

Tarun Jeevani
IG: tarun.jeevan
Tarun has done engineering and left his job to support his family. He is truthful by nature and a good listener. Listening to you.